Dog Food

by Elizabeth Best

illustrated by Cliff Watt

⊤

The Characters

Mrs Gladys McTavish

Mutt
Gladys' dog

Joan
Gladys' daughter

Dave
Gladys' son

The Setting

Fleet Street

Ruffian Road

Ring Road

Old Manns Road

Rupert's Farm

To Lockys Lookout

1 3 5 7 9 11 13 15 17 19 21 23

Hillery Street

Mrs McTavish's Place

Bottle Park

Mountains

Ring Road

Brush Park

Railway Station

Mt Edmund

to Crumbletown

Railway Road

MARTY'S Supermarket

Dead Dog Corner

Luny Avenue

Sweet Street

Oval Road

Muttley Street

South Park

Rocky Road

Howard's Island

White River

Point Snobby

Town of Fairweather

Willow Creek

to Rumble Creek

Mt Burly-Burly

CONTENTS

CHAPTER  1

Shopping

Mrs Gladys McTavish was very old. She lived on her own.

Her only friend was her dog, Mutt
Mutt was an odd-looking dog.

He only had one eye
and a little stump of a tail.
But Mrs McTavish loved him.

Each week Mrs McTavish
went shopping at the supermarket.

The very first thing
she would pick up
was dog food for Mutt.

Then she would choose
her own food.

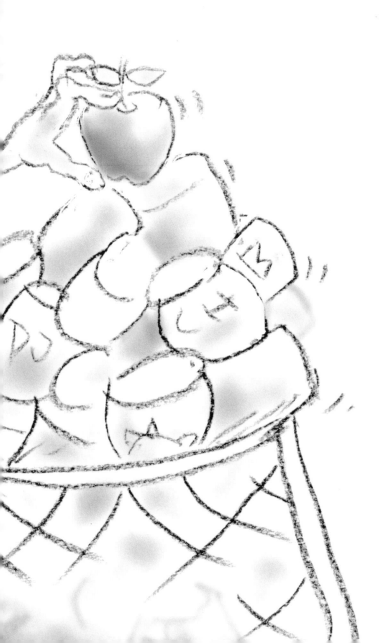

CHAPTER  2

Dinner Time

At dinner time, Mrs McTavish
watched Mutt wolfing down
his dog food.

His bit-of-a-tail wagged furiously.
His one eye gleamed.
Mutt couldn't wait to finish the lot

Mrs McTavish was envious.
"Why don't I enjoy my food
like that?"

She had a great idea.

"I'll buy some dog food for myself," she thought.

So, for the next few days,
Gladys ate dog food for dinner.

"It's delicious," Mrs McTavish said to Mutt. "Why didn't I think of this before?"

CHAPTER  3

Dogs Have Their Ways

One day an awful thing happened.

Mrs McTavish bit Bill the Postman on the leg.

"Stop it!" cried Bill.
"Why are you biting me?"

Mrs McTavish stopped.
She looked at Bill,
her friendly postman.

"I beg your pardon," she said.
"I am sorry."

Then she went back inside.

Mrs Gladys McTavish was puzzled
by what she had done.
But soon she forgot all about it.

Bill the Postman didn't forget.
His leg hurt. So he wrote a letter
to Mrs McTavish's daughter, Joan.

"I'm not a difficult man," he wrote
"but if your Mum's so hungry
that she needs to bite my leg,
I think you'd better come."

"That's not like Mum," Joan thought,
as she read the letter.
"Mum always liked vegetables more
than meat."

Joan decided to pay her mother
a visit.

CHAPTER 4

Dogs and Cats

A few days later, Mrs McTavish
chased her neighbour's cat up a tree.

This time Gladys was surprised by
her own behaviour. Fluffy, the cat
was even more surprised.

The most surprised was Mr Brown, Fluffy's owner.

"Oy!" Mr Brown yelled.
"Leave Fluffy alone! What has she
ever done to you?"

"I beg your pardon,"
said Mrs Gladys McTavish,
as she hurried into her house.

CHAPTER  5

Another Letter

That night Mr Brown wrote
a letter to Mrs McTavish's son,
Dave.

"You'd better do something about
your Mum," he wrote. "She's not
herself."

When Dave read the letter
he was puzzled.

"If Mum's not herself, who is she?

Dave decided to pay his mother
a visit.

On the same day
and at the same time
Dave and Joan arrived
at the railway station.

37

They shared a taxi to take them to their mother's house.

As they drove into Mrs McTavish's
street, a small grey figure
dashed out into the road.

It barked and bit at the tyres
of the taxi.

It was Mrs Gladys McTavish!

CHAPTER  6

One Bark Too Many

The taxi screeched to a stop.
Dave and Joan leapt out.

"Mum!" they cried. "What are
you doing?"

"Ruuufff!" said Mrs McTavish, as an empty can of dog food fell out of her pocket.

"Yum," she said. "I like dog food."

The shocking news went up
and down the street.

"This must stop at once," bellowed the butcher.

"It isn't allowed," shouted
the shopkeeper.

"No dog food," the police officer sa[id],
"or I'll have to lock you up."

48

"You'll get sick," said the doctor.

"Stop now!" cried the teacher.

At last Mrs Gladys McTavish gave in.

"All right," she said sadly, "I'll stop eating dog food."

Everyone cheered.

Dave went home and Joan went home.

A few days passed.
Mrs McTavish was bored.

As she was walking through
the supermarket, she stopped.

She looked at the shelf.

"That cat food looks nice,"
said Mrs Gladys McTavish.

GLOSSARY

awful
very bad

bellowed
shouted loudly

dashed
ran quickly

envious
to want what
someone else has

furiously
unstoppable energy

I beg your pardon
a polite way of
saying sorry

puzzled
to think about
a problem

wolfing
to eat very quickly

Elizabeth Best

Elizabeth Best writes a bit of everything ... adult short stories, children's stories, plays, articles and novels.
Best of all though, she enjoys writing stories for children. It is pure joy!

Cliff Watt

I started illustrating after I became shipwrecked on a desert island. It was very difficult at first, but soon I learnt to use everything. This book was drawn with a burnt bone from last night's dinner.